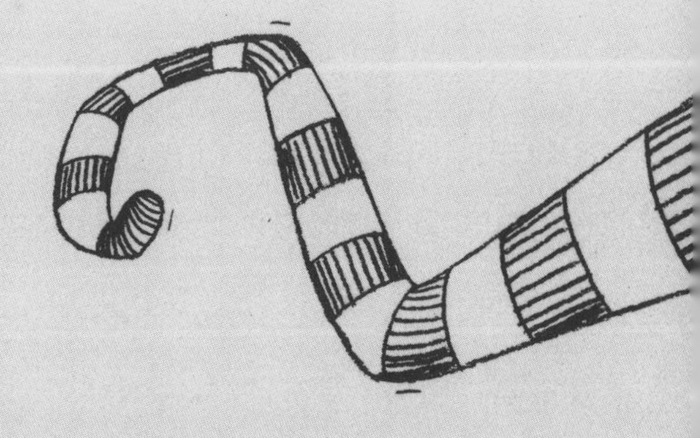

the Three Grumpies

Alex, Ben and David—your laughter keeps my Grumpies away. –T.W.

For Tom and Ette –R.C.

Type design by Ross Collins

First U.S. Edition 2003
Published by Bloomsbury, New York and London
Distributed to the trade by Holtzbrinck Publishers
Library of Congress Cataloging-in-Publication Data:
Wight, Tamra.
The three grumpies / by Tamra Wight; illustrated by Ross Collins.
p. cm.
Summary: A little girl wakes up with the grumpies, three of them in fact, who follow her around all day causing trouble, until she figures out how to get rid of them.
ISBN 1-58234-840-5
[1. Mood (Psychology)--Fiction.] I. Collins, Ross, ill. II. Title.
PZ7.W63935 Th 2003
[E]--dc21
2002028345

Color separation by SC (Sang Choy) International
Printed in Hong Kong

1 3 5 7 9 10 8 6 4 2

Bloomsbury USA Children's Books
175 Fifth Avenue
New York, New York 10010

the Three Grumpies

by Tamra Wight illustrated by Ross Collins

I woke up on the wrong side of the bed this morning.

Grumpy,

Grumpier

and Grumpiest
were waiting for me.

"Oh my!"
said Mom.
"It looks like you
have the Grumpies
today.

Try to get
rid of them,
dear."

So I yelled,
GO AWAY!
The Grumpies
just smiled.
All three
of them.

Grumpy jiggled the table
until my milk spilled.
I shouted, GET OUT!
Grumpier
squeezed
toothpaste
everywhere.

Grumpiest hid one shoe from every pair I own.
I hollered,
I MEAN IT!
I couldn't get rid of them.

"Dad, I have the Grumpies today!"

"Try showing them how you feel," Dad suggested.

So I stamped my foot and pointed to the door.

I tried to make my lunch, but Grumpy had eaten all the snacks.

I shook my fist at him.

I tried to pack my homework, but Grumpier had lost it.

I stuck my tongue out at him.

Grumpiest tripped me as I got on the bus.

SCHOOL BUS
Showing them how
I felt wasn't working.

"Mr. Little,
I have the
Grumpies today."
"Try scaring them away,"
said my bus driver.

So I put on my
meanest face.

The Grumpies giggled.

All three of them.

At school
Grumpy broke
all my
favorite
crayons.
Then
Grumpier
squished
my lunch
flat.
In art Grumpiest
splattered paint
on my new shirt.

I frowned at him.
I glared at him.
Mean faces were not working.

"Miss Gray," I said.
"I have the Grumpies today."
"Try ignoring them,"
said my teacher.
So I
turned
my back
on them.

The Grumpies smiled. All three of them.

Grumpy tripped me as I got off the bus.

Grumpier kept

I looked to the right and hummed.

stealing my hat.
Grumpiest dropped my homework in a puddle.
I looked to the left and whistled.
Ignoring them wasn't working.

"Mom, the Grumpies are still here!"

"Oh dear!" said Mom. She looked a little frazzled.

I smiled a little weary smile.

But the Grumpies didn't smile.
In fact they looked a little
nervous.

All three of them.

So... when Grumpy made mud in the sandbox,

I giggled at him.

When Grumpier dumped my green beans on the floor,

I chuckled at him.
When Grumpiest poured the whole bottle of soap in the tub,
I fell down laughing!

The next thing I knew, the Grumpies were waving goodbye.

All three of them.

"What a grumpy day," I said to Mom
as she kissed
me goodnight.

I wonder who
will get the Grumpies next?